P9-DNK-722

# Seriously, Just Go to Sleep

by Adam Mansbach

illustrated by Ricardo Cortés

E
Mansbach,
Adam

Published by Akashic Books
Words ©2012 Adam Mansbach
Illustrations ©2012 Ricardo Cortés

ISBN-13: 978-1-61775-078-6
Library of Congress Control Number: 2011960952
First printing

Akashic Books
PO Box 1456
New York, NY 10009
info@akashicbooks.com
www.akashicbooks.com

**Adam Mansbach**'s books include a beloved, bad-word-filled "children's" book our publisher won't let us name here, as well as the California Book Award–winning novel *The End of the Jews*, the cult classic *Angry Black White Boy*, and the graphic novel *Nature of the Beast*. His new novel, *Rage Is Back*, will be published in January 2013.

www.AdamMansbach.com

In addition to the aforementioned unmentionable, **Ricardo Cortés** has illustrated books about grass, jury duty, electricity, and the Jamaican bobsled team. He lives in Brooklyn, where he is working on a book about a shark.

www.RMCortes.com

*to all the children . . .*
*may your kids bring you as much joy as you've brought us*

The cats nestle close to their kittens,
The lambs have lain down with the sheep.
You're cozy and warm in your bed, my dear.
Please, just this once, go to sleep.

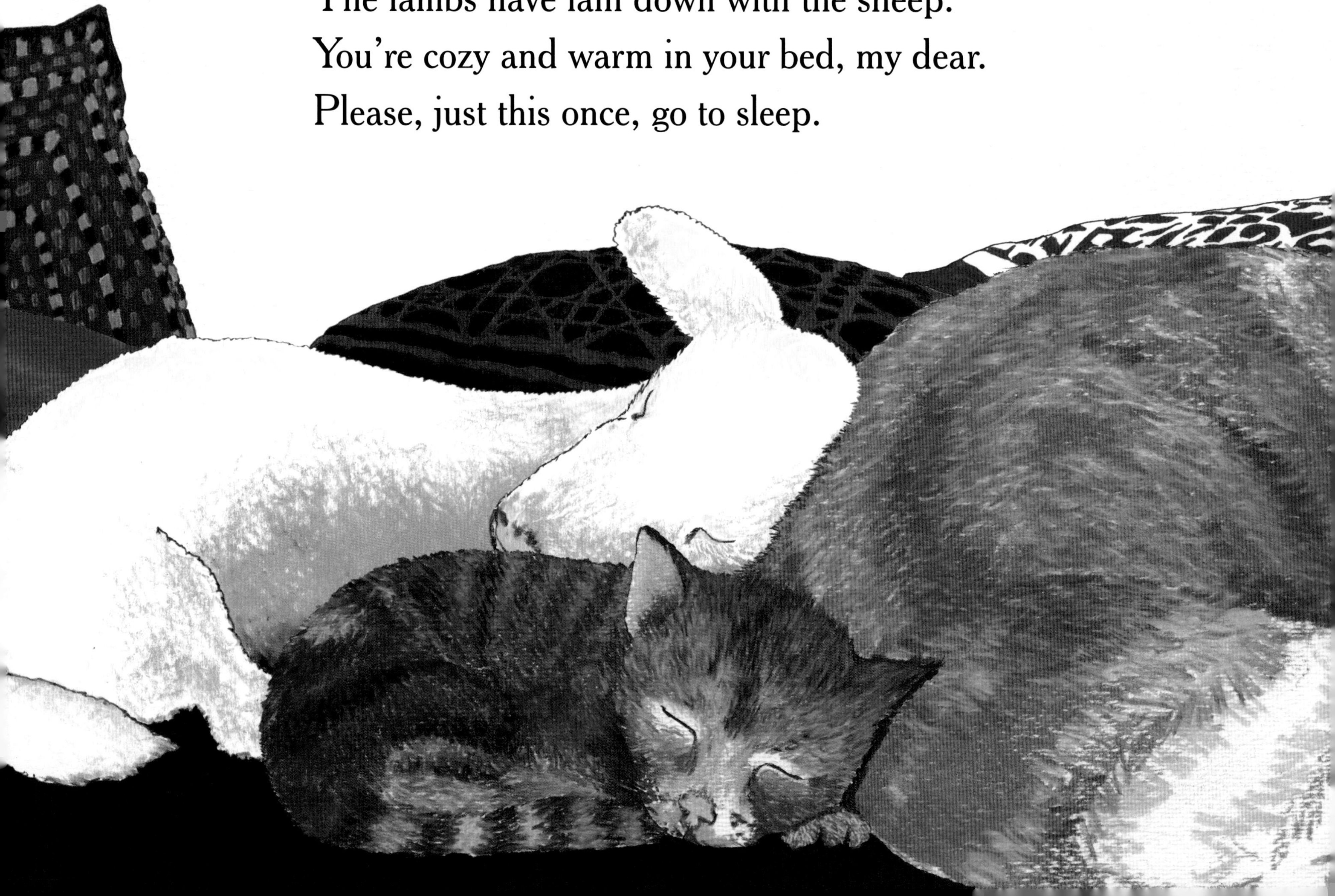

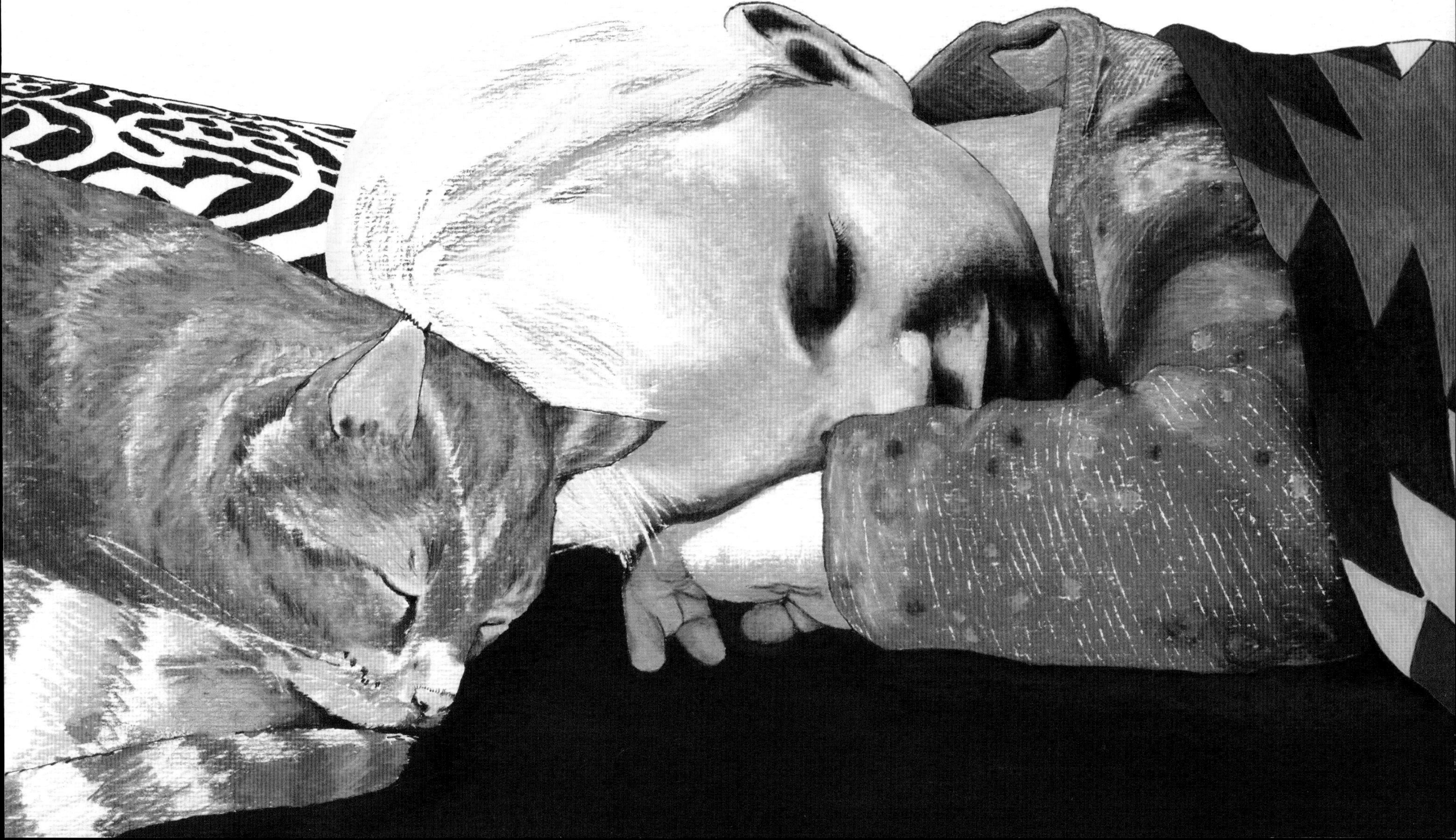

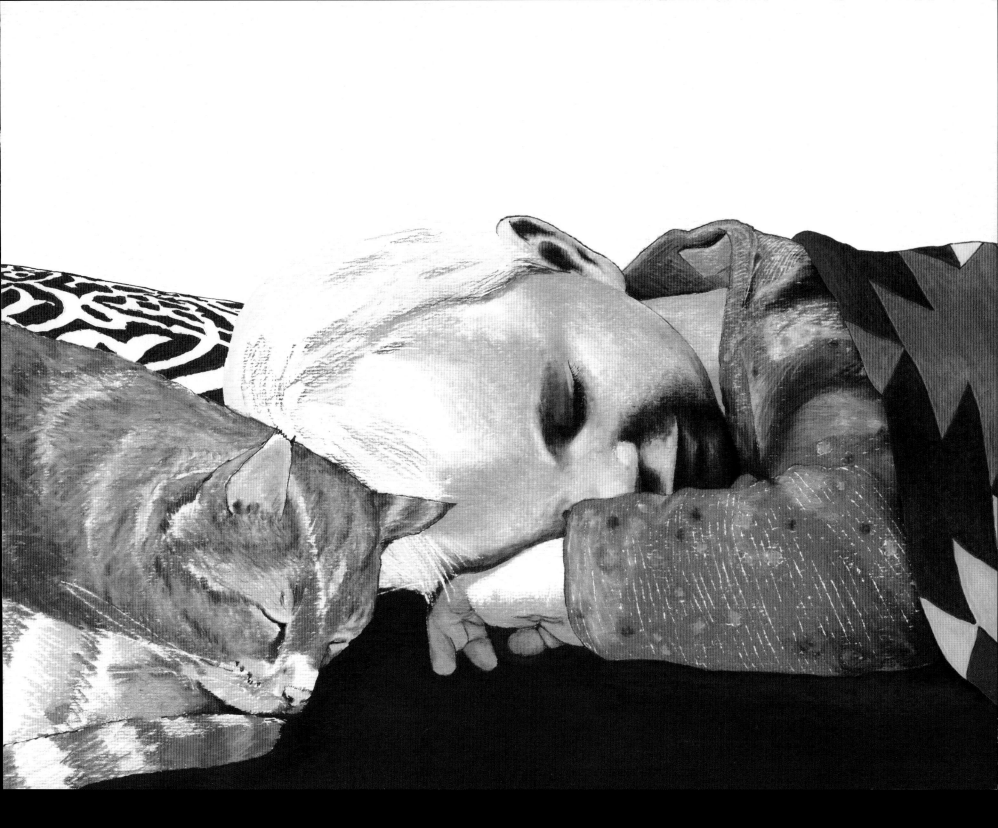

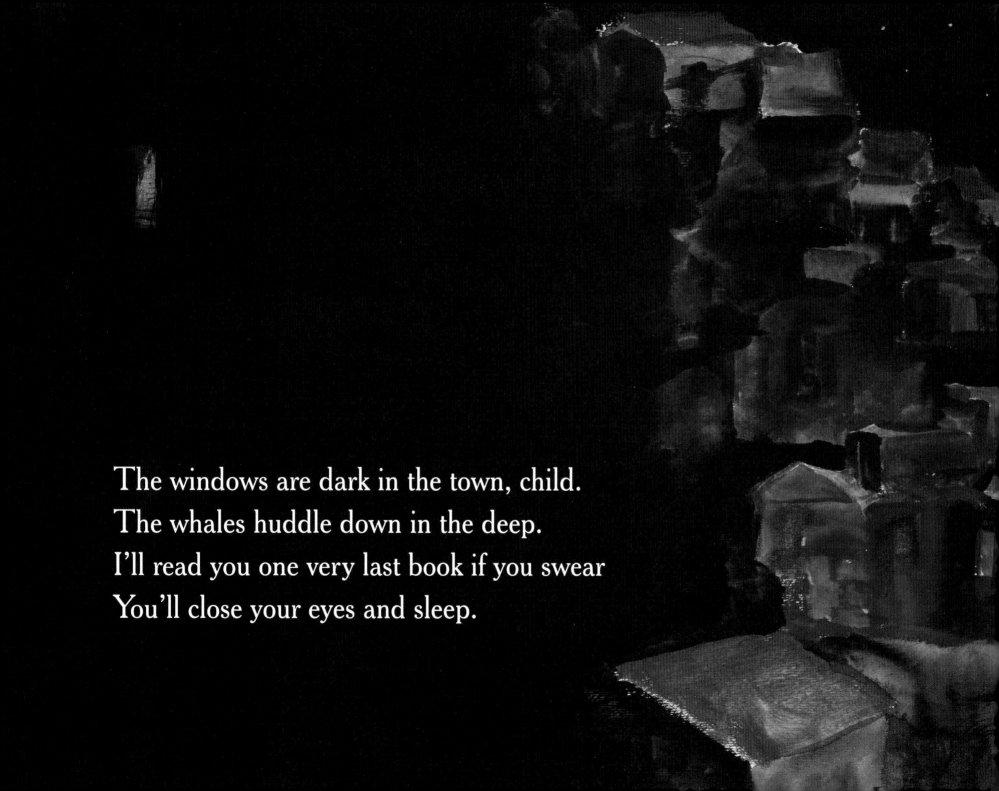

The windows are dark in the town, child.
The whales huddle down in the deep.
I'll read you one very last book if you swear
You'll close your eyes and sleep.

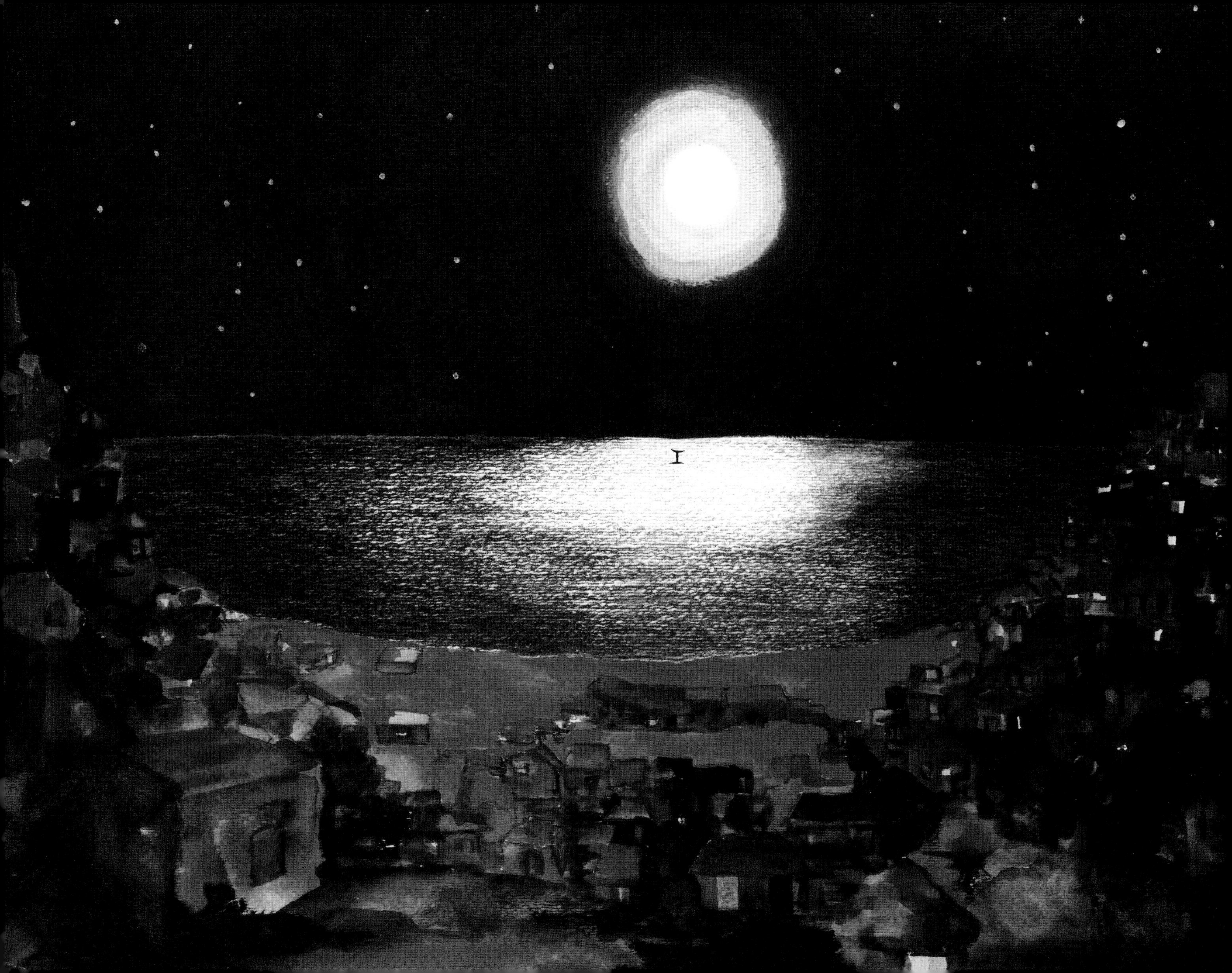

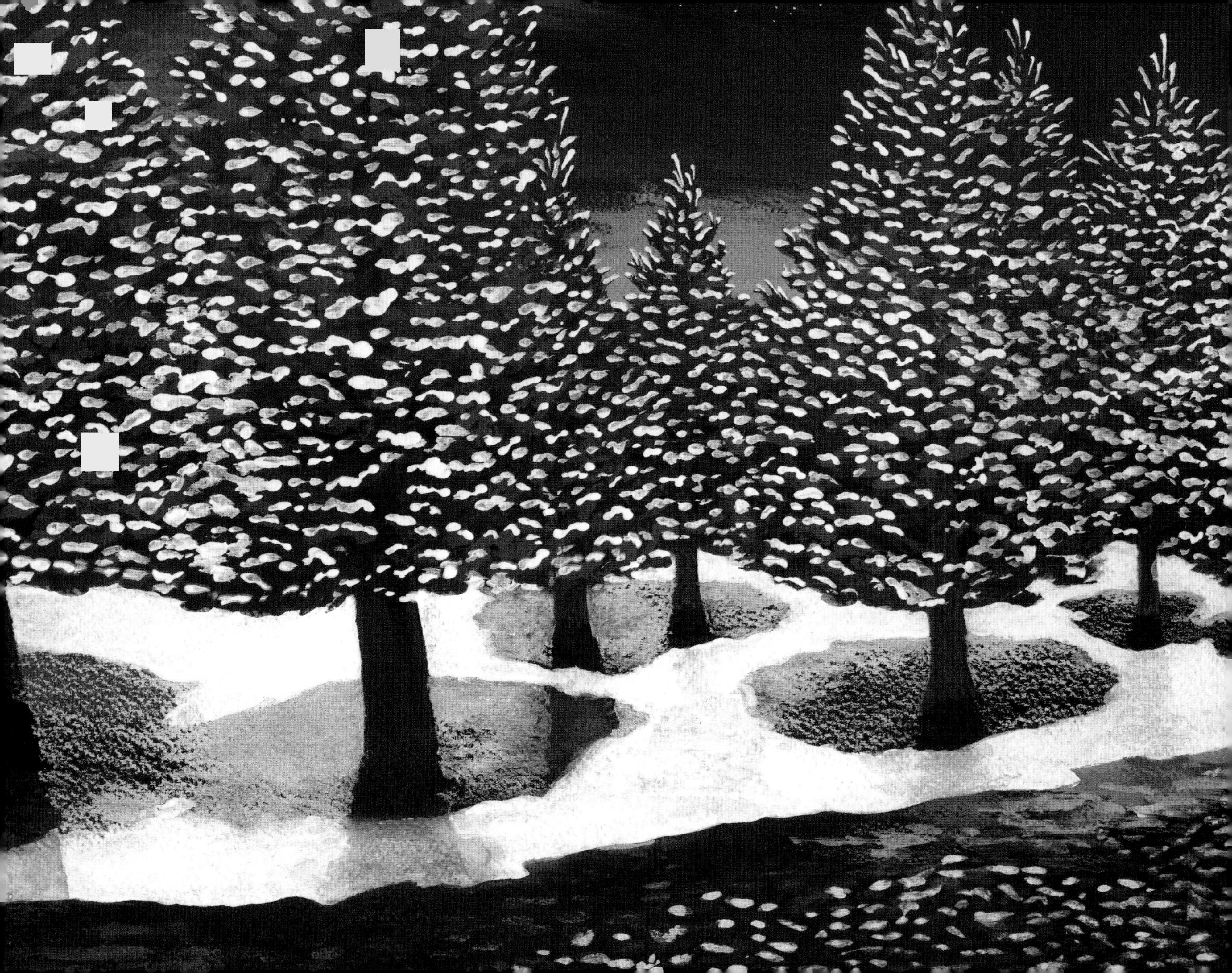

The eagles who soar through the sky are at rest
And the creatures who crawl, run, and creep.
I know you're not thirsty. You just had a drink.
Stop goofing around now, and sleep.

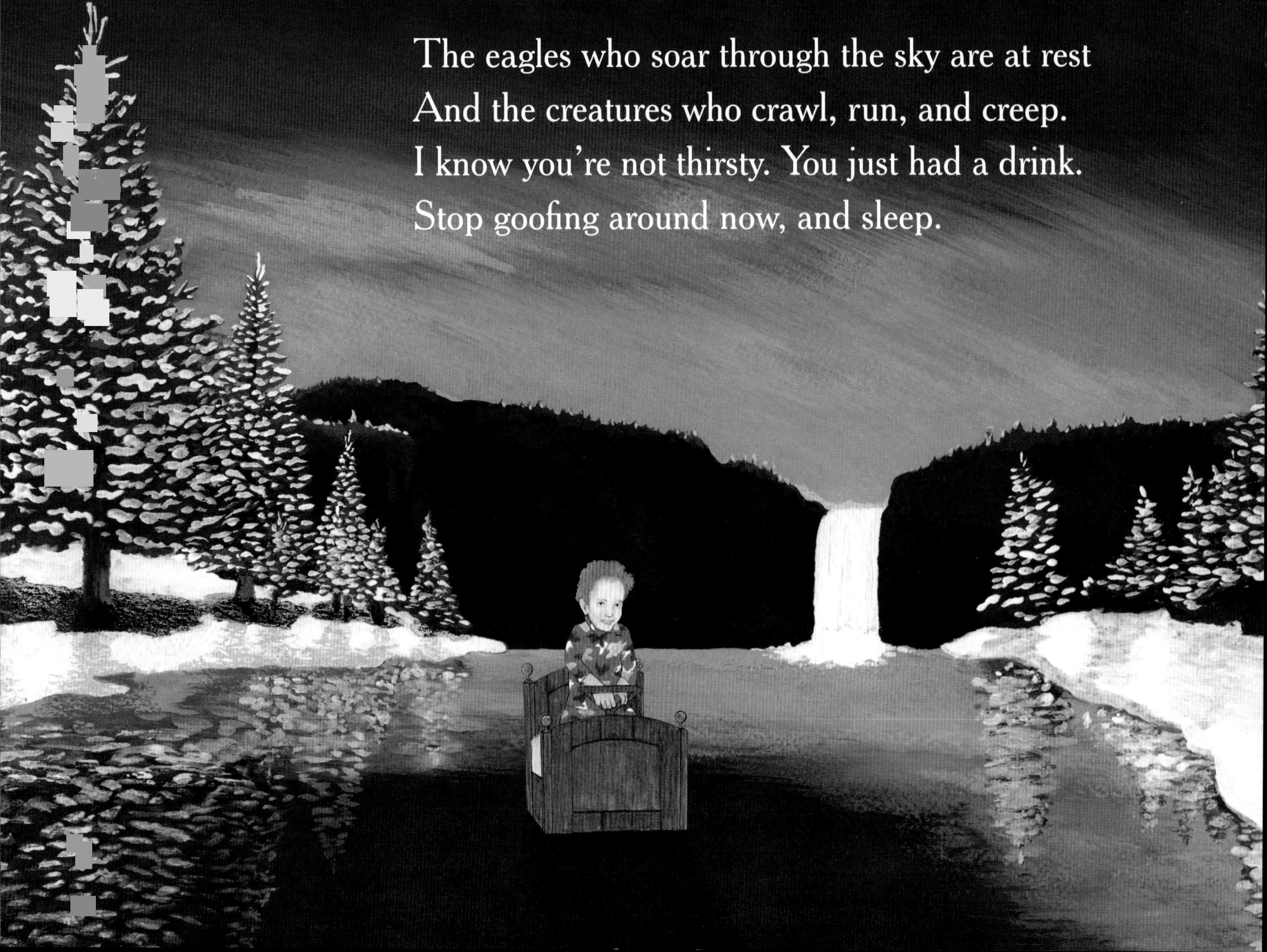

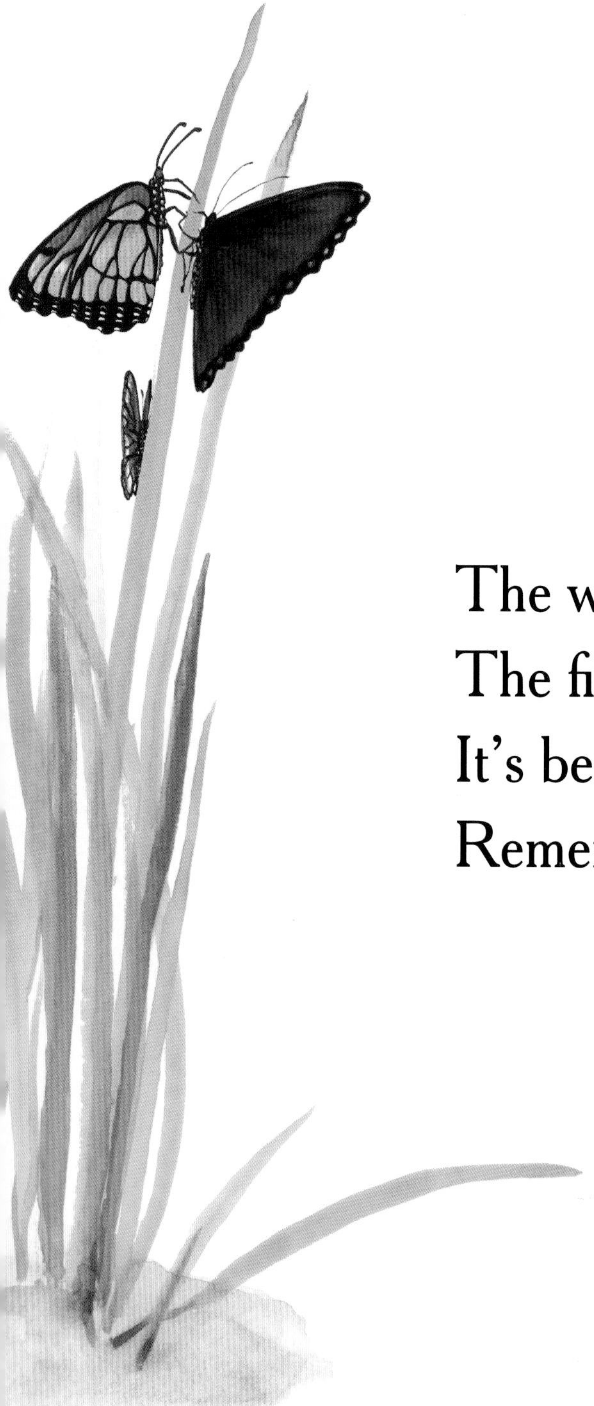

The wind whispers soft through the grass, hon.
The field mice, they make not a peep.
It's been thirty-eight minutes already.
Remember, we made a deal? Sleep.

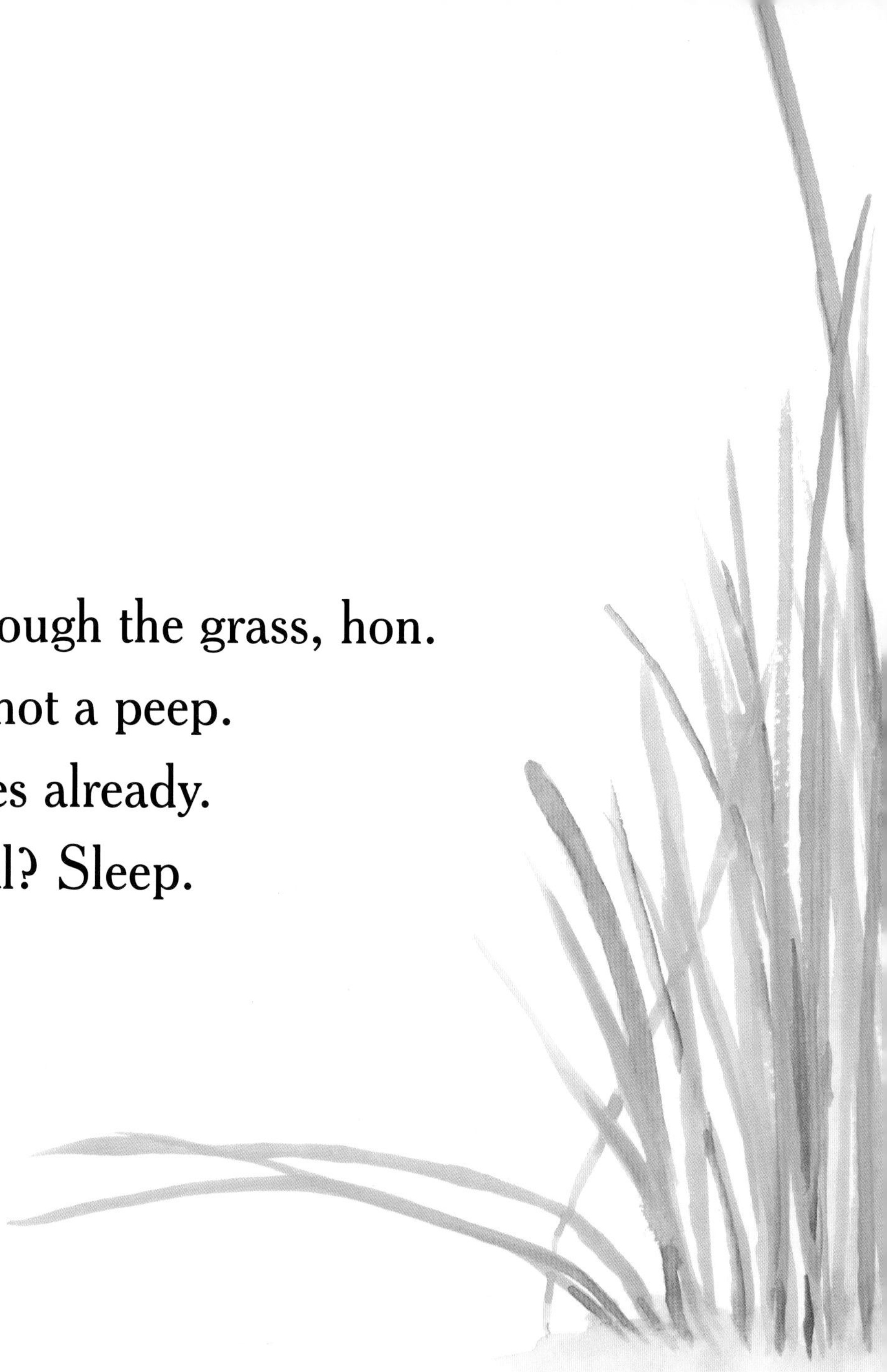

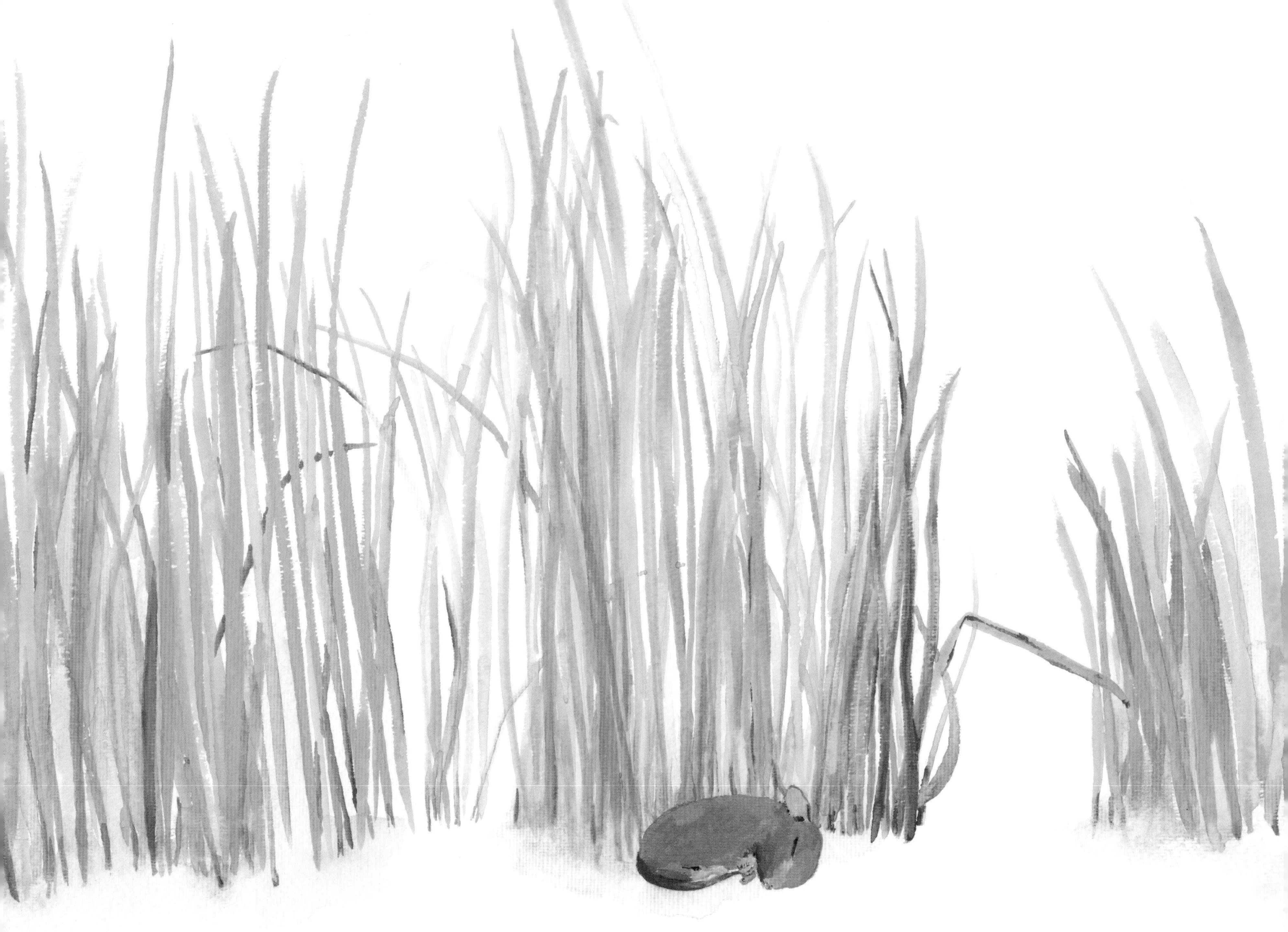

All the kids from preschool are in dreamland.
The froggie has made his last leap.
No way, you can't go to the bathroom.
Guess where you can go, my darling? To sleep.

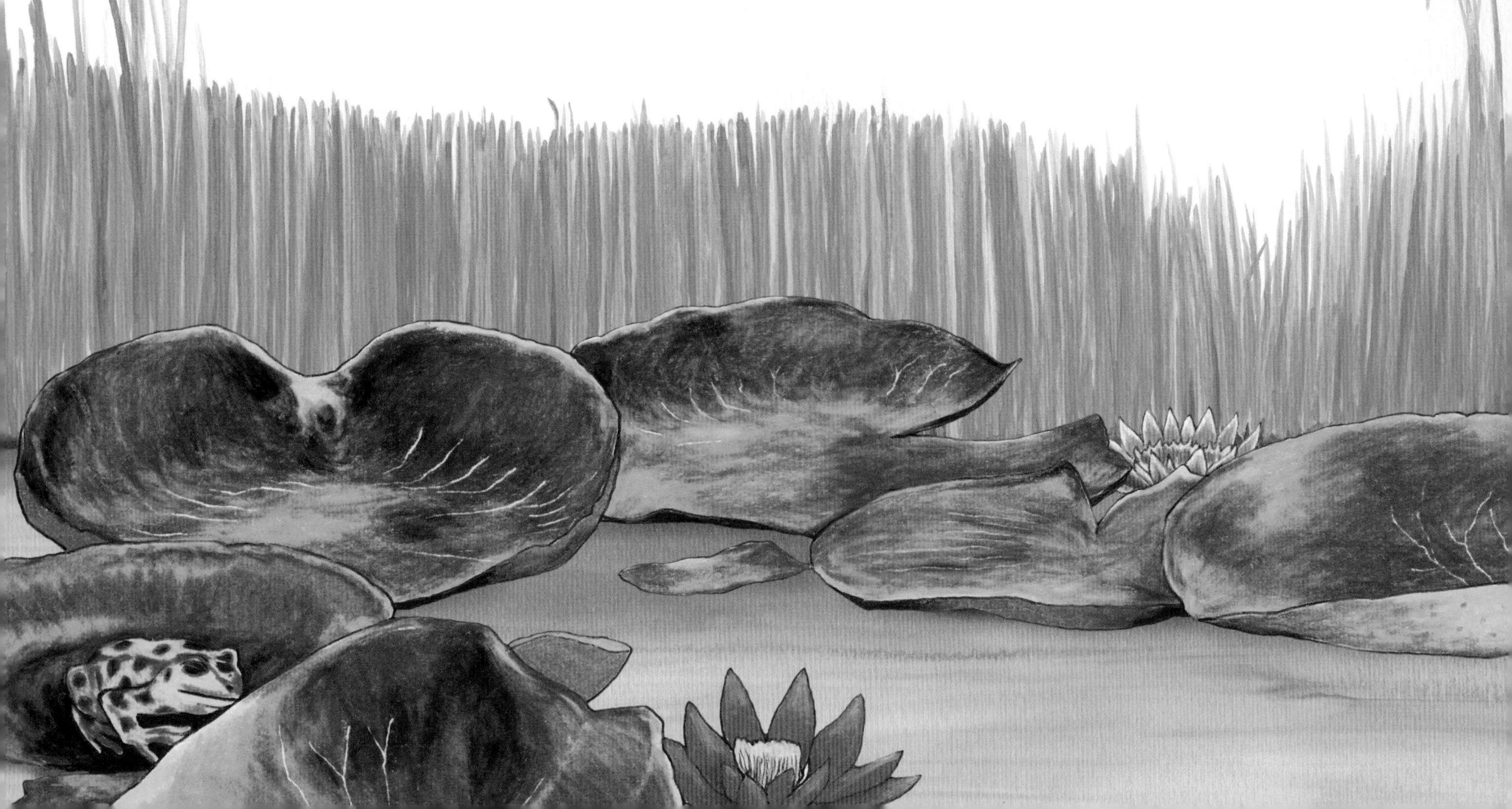

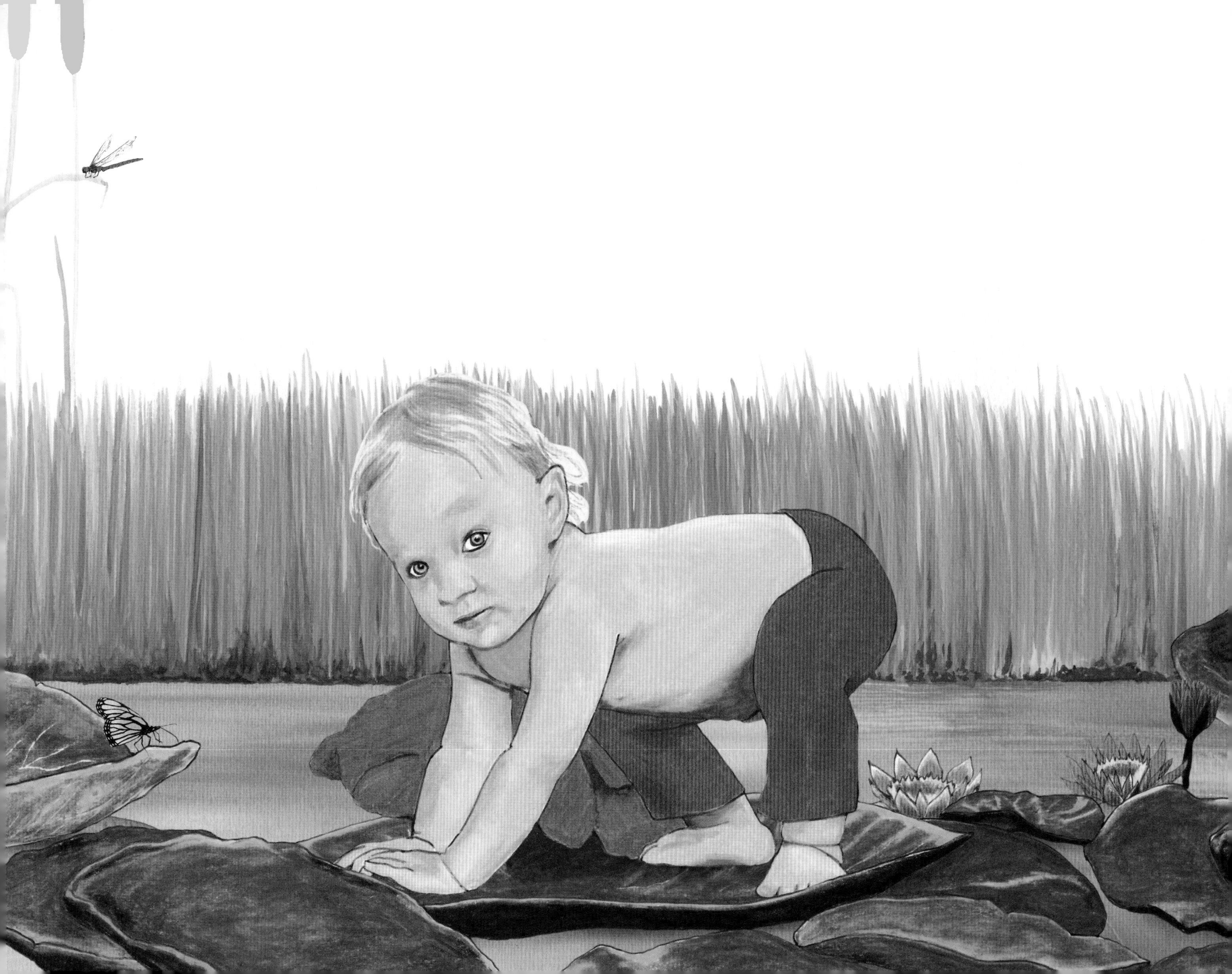

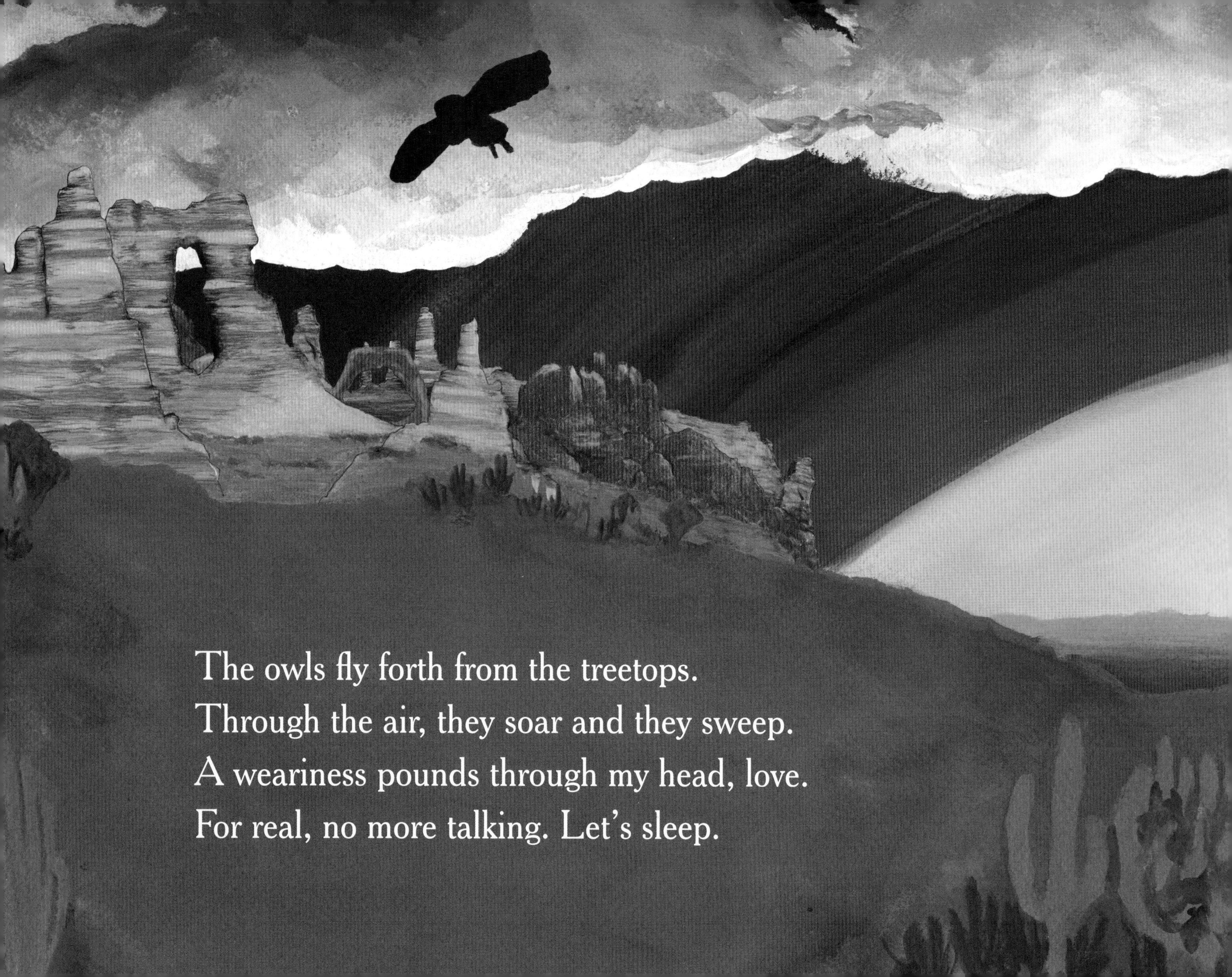

The owls fly forth from the treetops.
Through the air, they soar and they sweep.
A weariness pounds through my head, love.
For real, no more talking. Let's sleep.

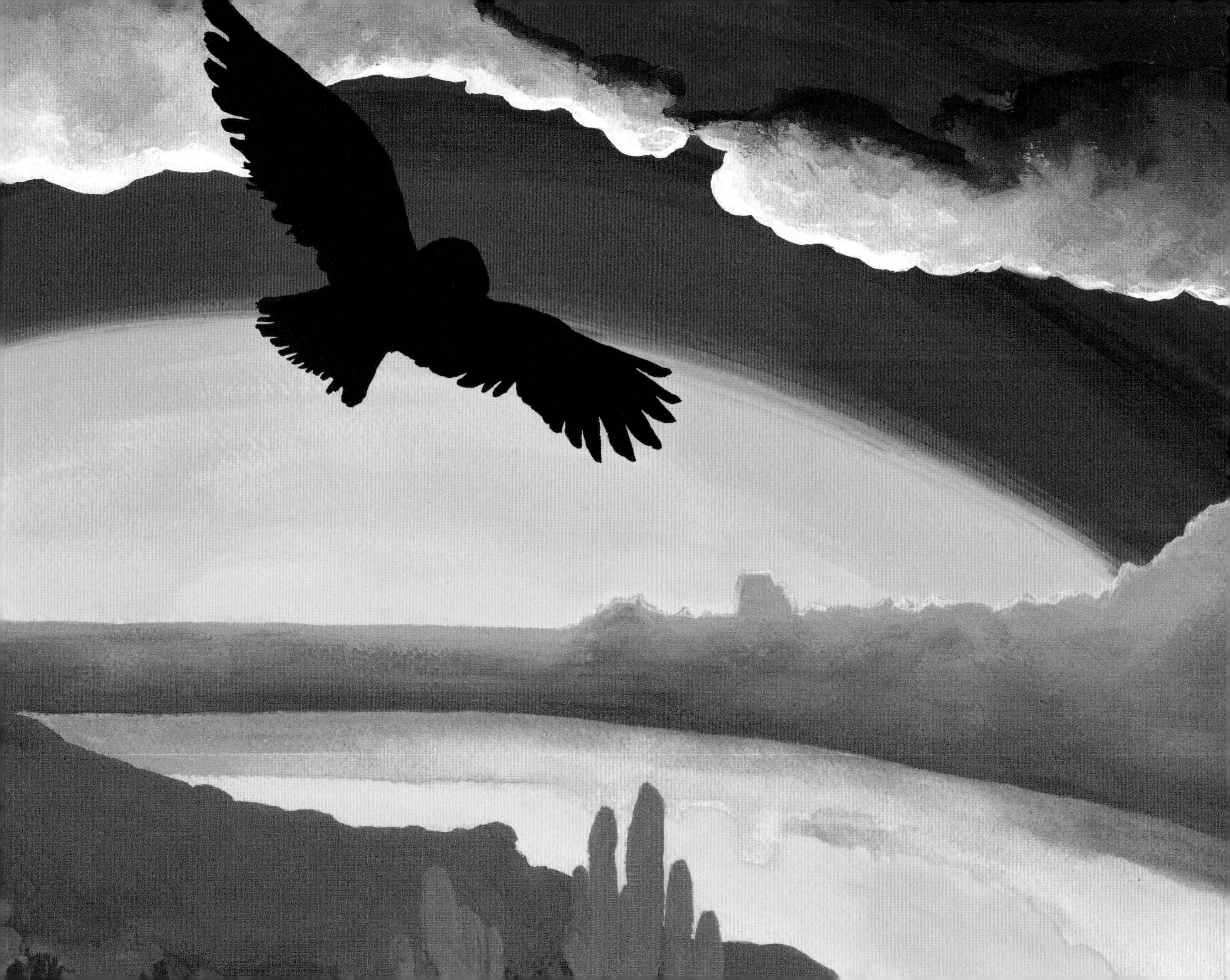

The cubs and the lions are snoring,
Wrapped in a big snuggly heap.
You're incredibly cute, and super-duper smart,
But why's it so hard to just sleep?

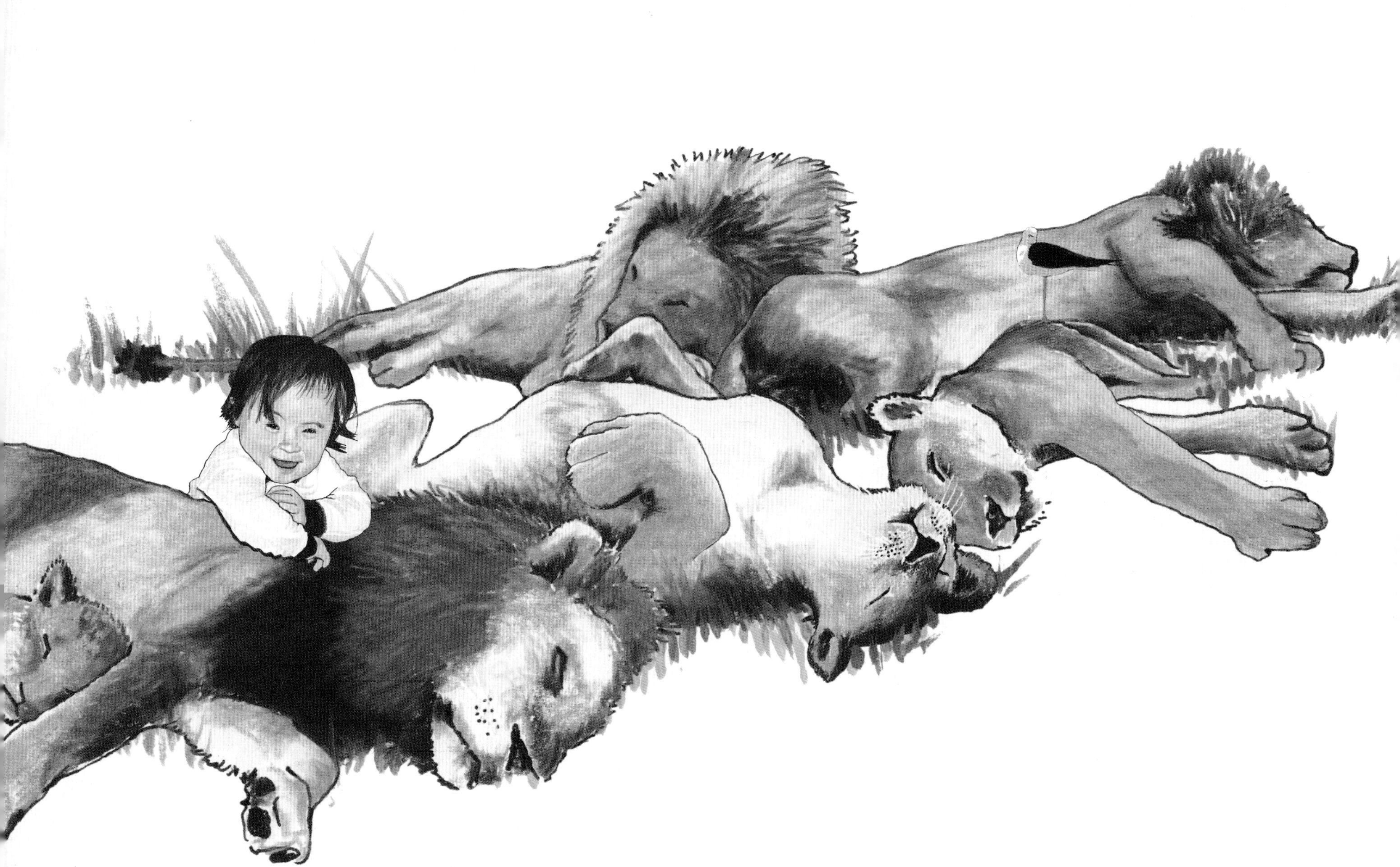

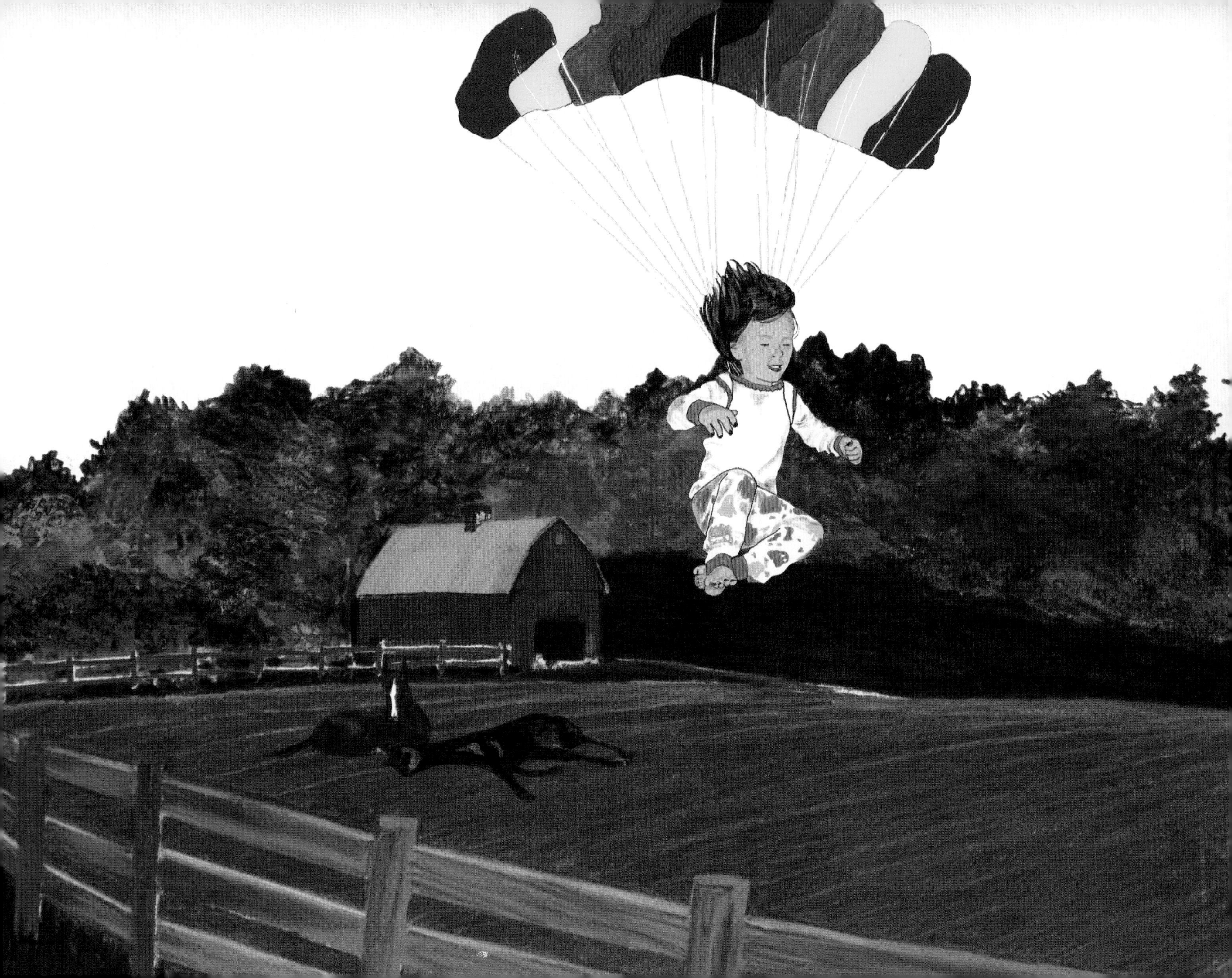

The seeds slumber beneath the earth now,
And the crops that the farmers will reap.
No more questions. This interview's over.
I've got three words for you, kid: go to sleep.

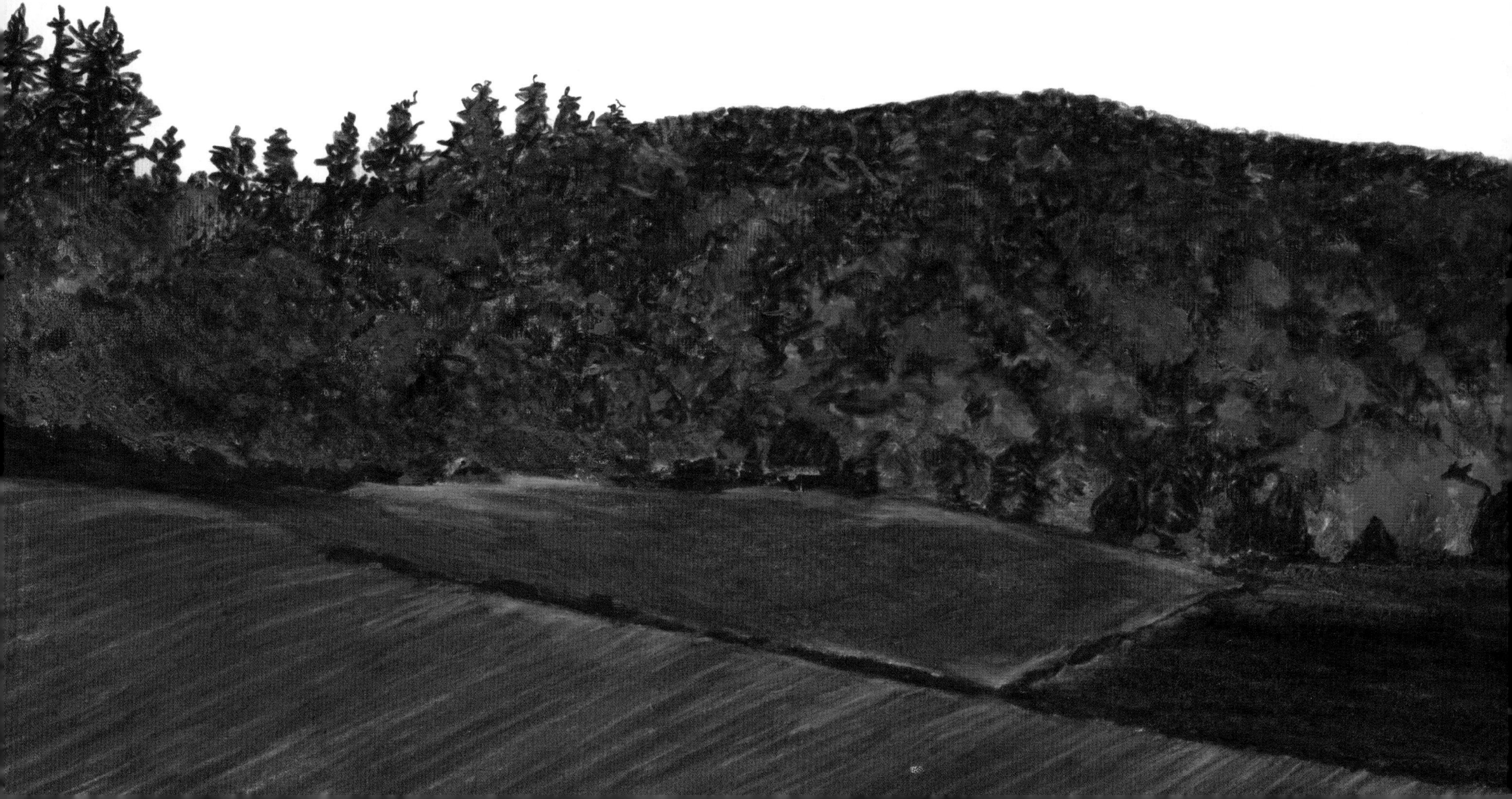

The tiger reclines in the simmering jungle.
The sparrow has silenced her cheep.
What do you want now? Another stuffed bear?
Four's plenty. Lie back down and sleep.

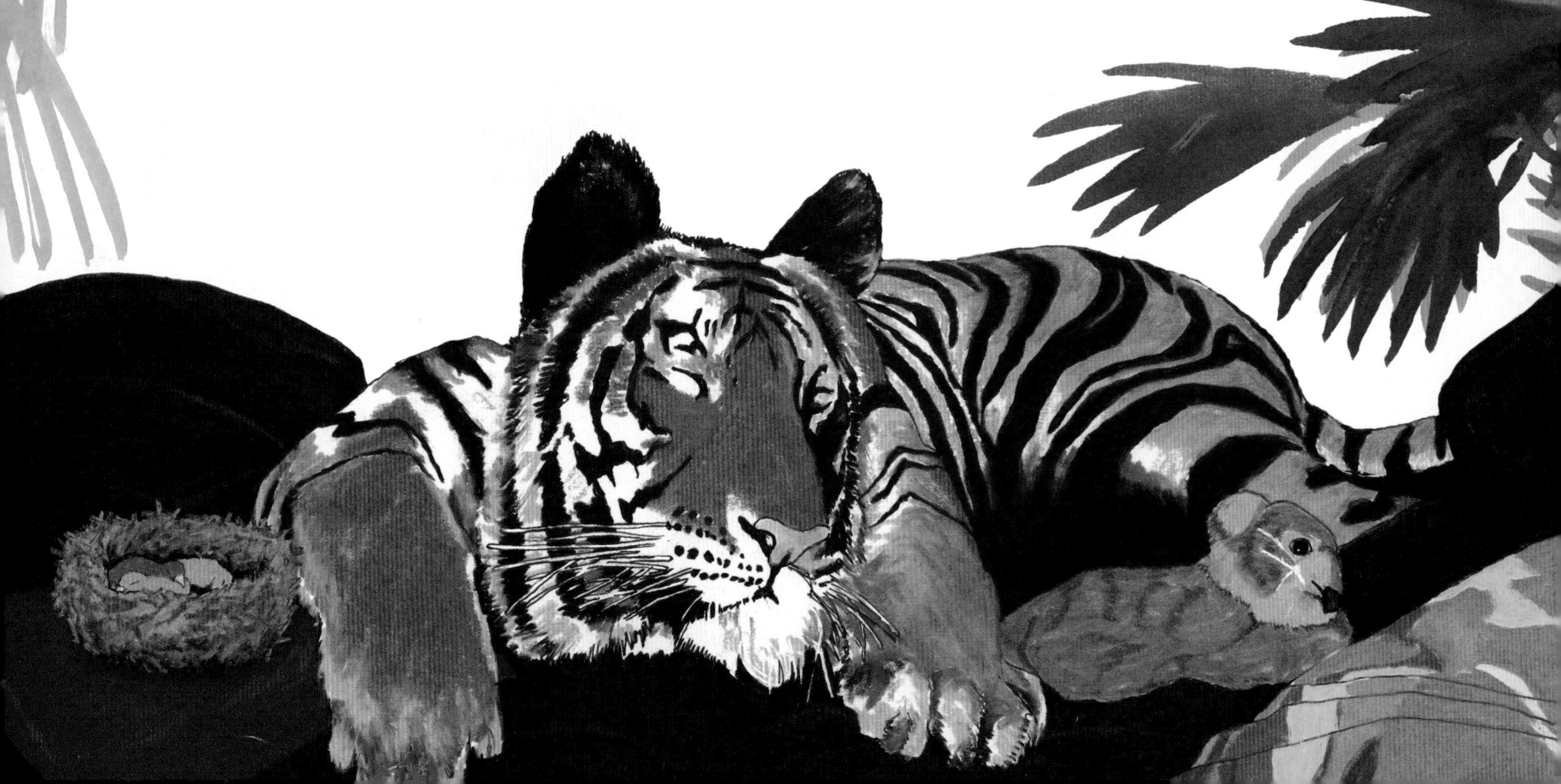

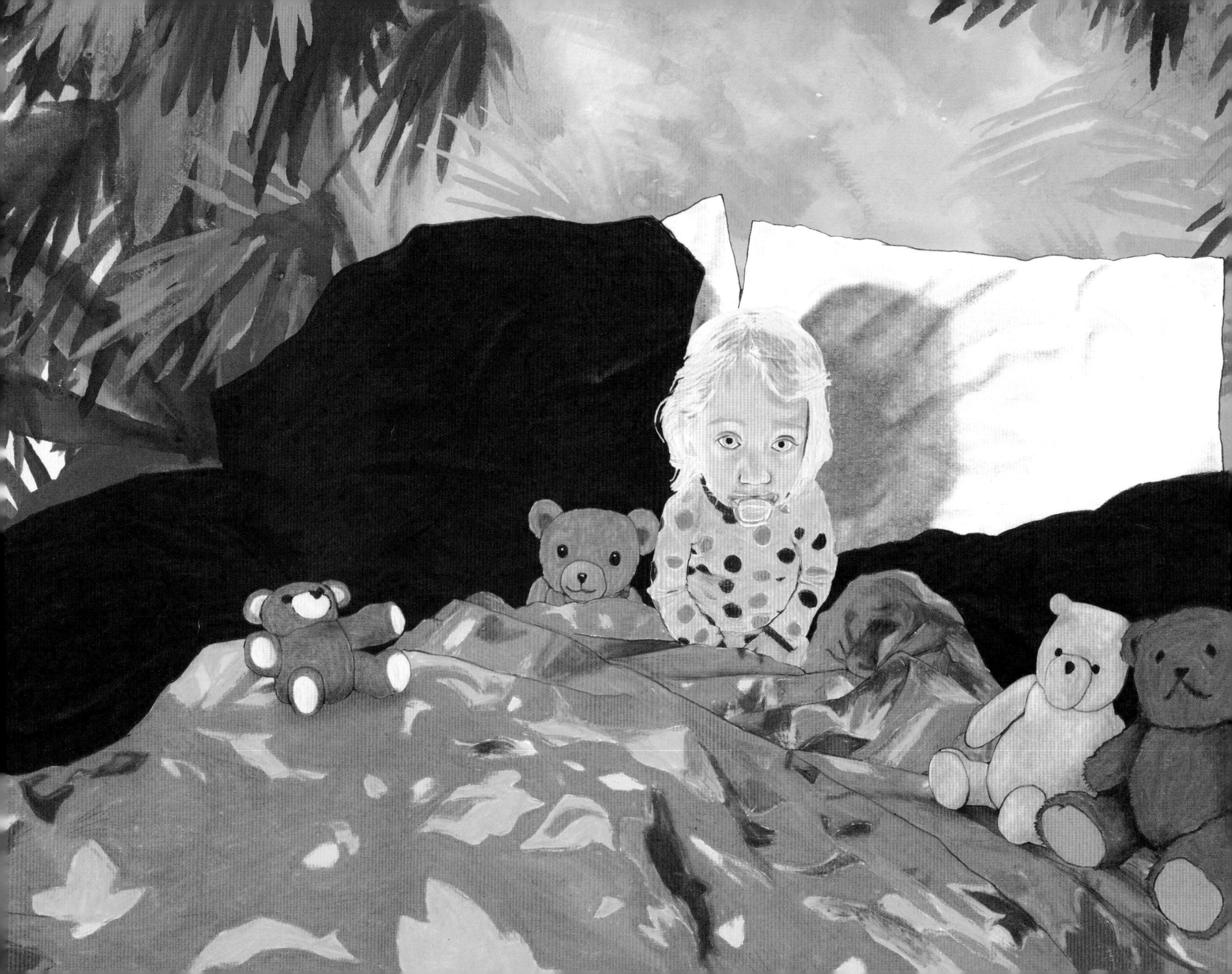

The flowers doze low in the meadows
And high on the mountains so steep.
My life is absurd. This is taking forever.
Stop messing with me, please, and sleep.

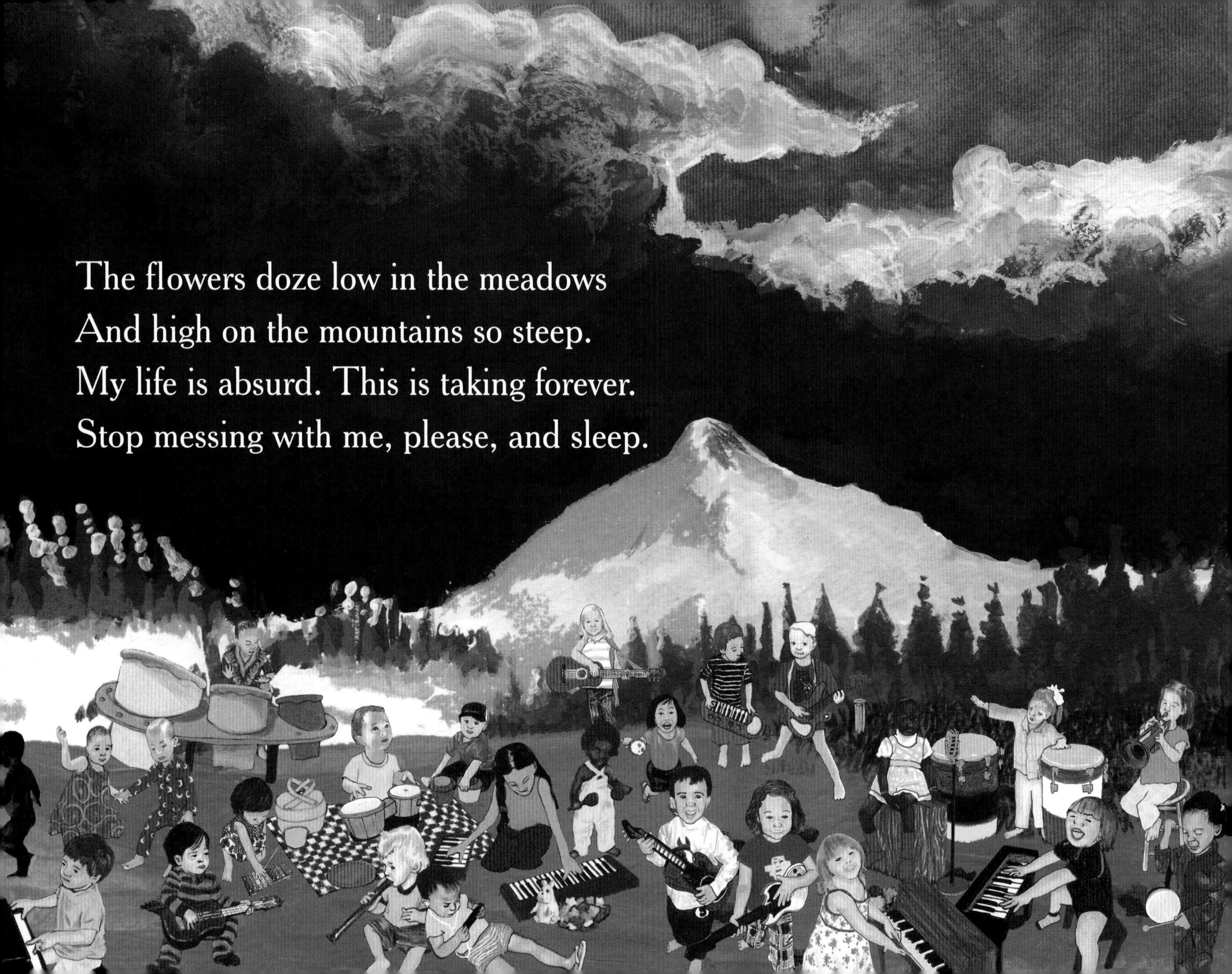

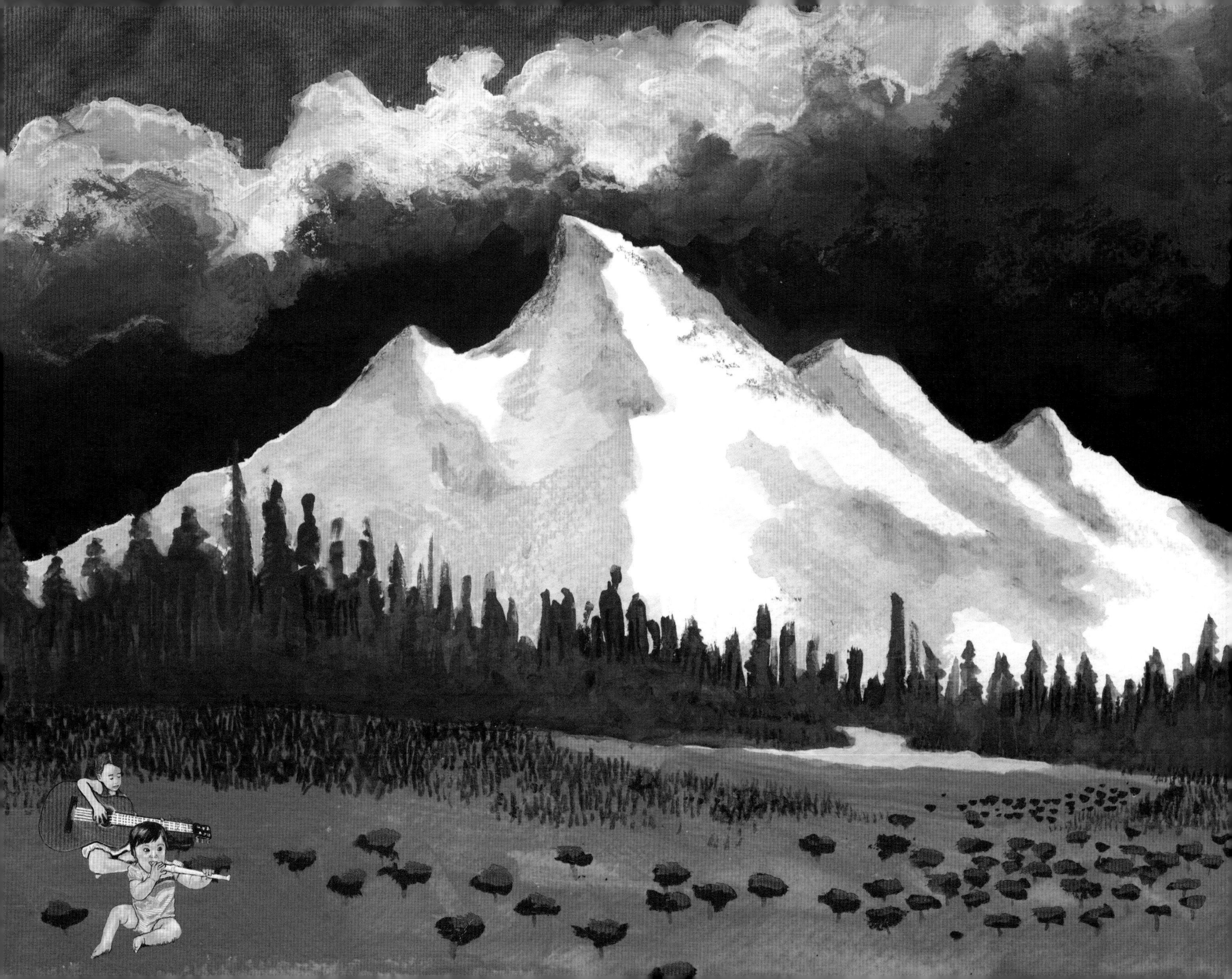

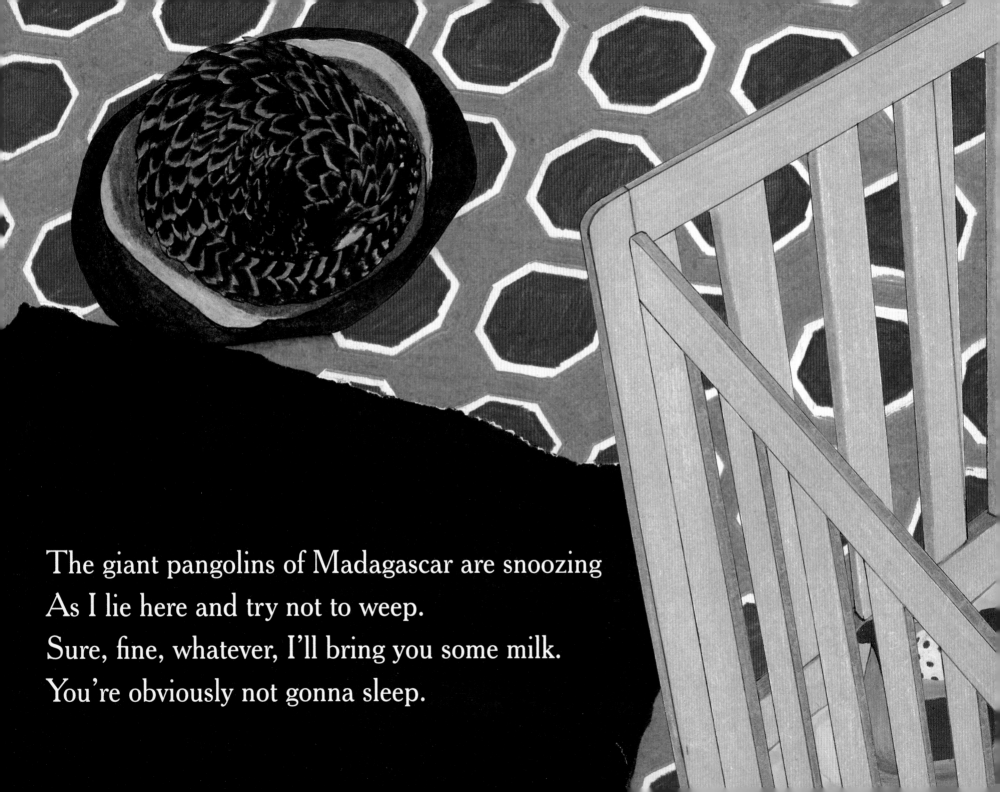

The giant pangolins of Madagascar are snoozing
As I lie here and try not to weep.
Sure, fine, whatever, I'll bring you some milk.
You're obviously not gonna sleep.

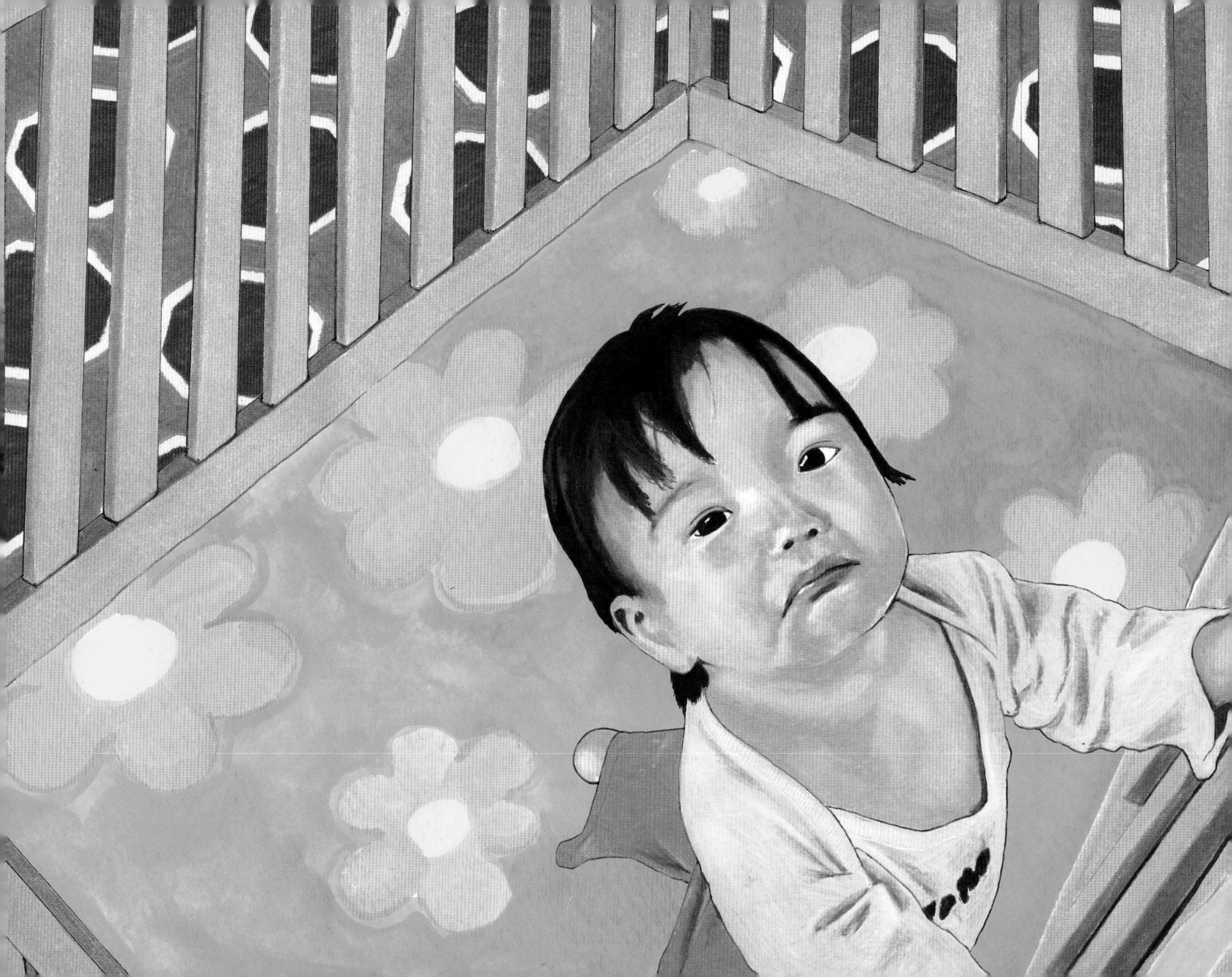

This room is all I can remember,
The furniture flimsy and cheap.
You win. You escape. You run down the hall.
As my chin hits my chest, and I sleep.

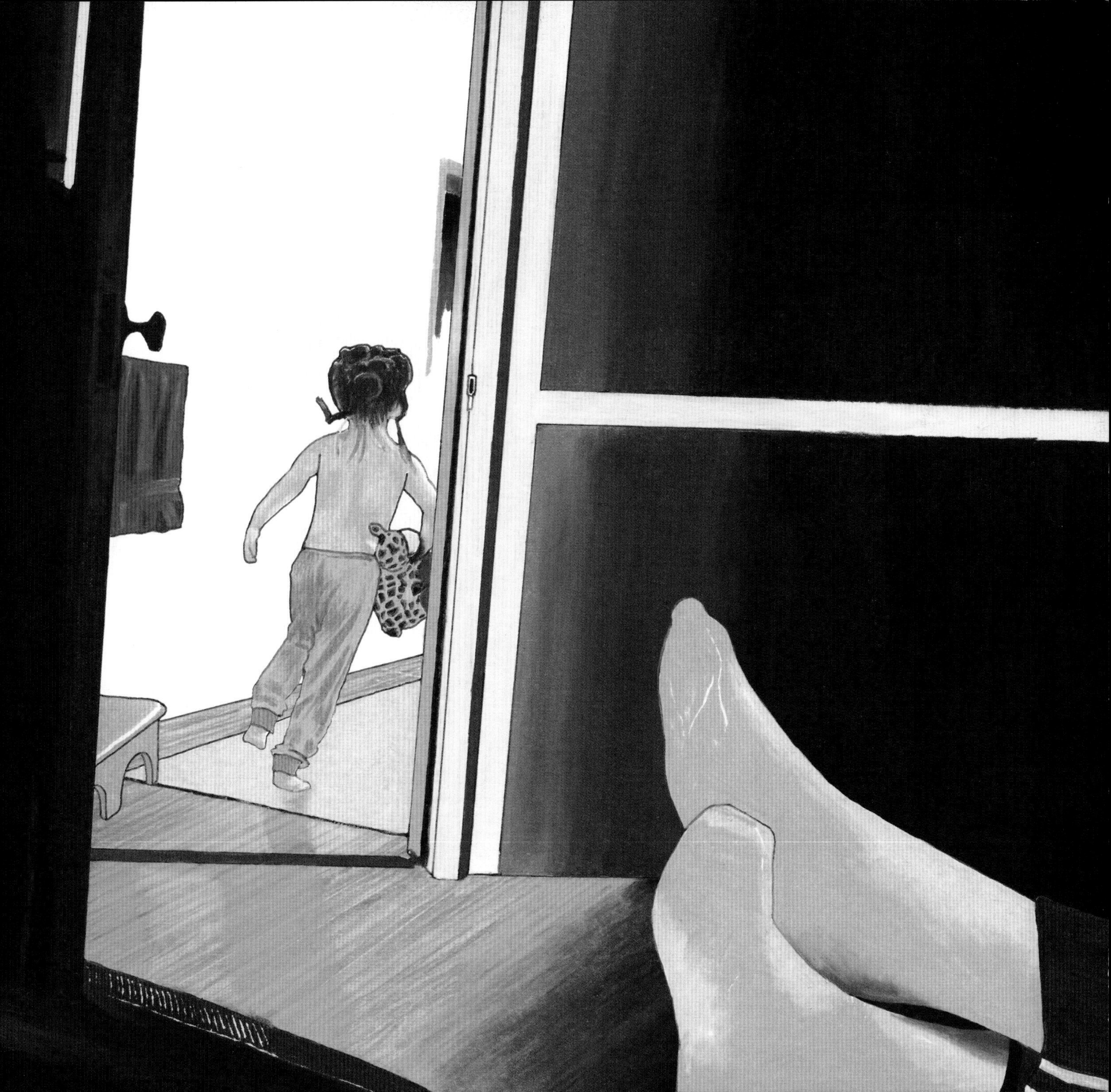

Bleary and dazed I awaken
To find your eyes shut, so I keep
My fingers crossed tight as I tiptoe away
And pray that you're really asleep.

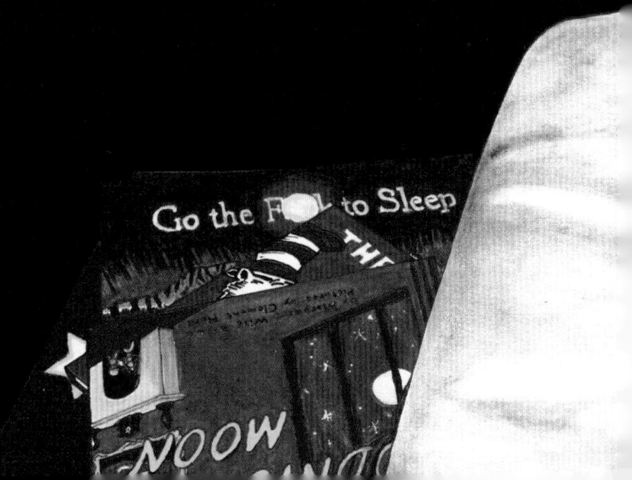

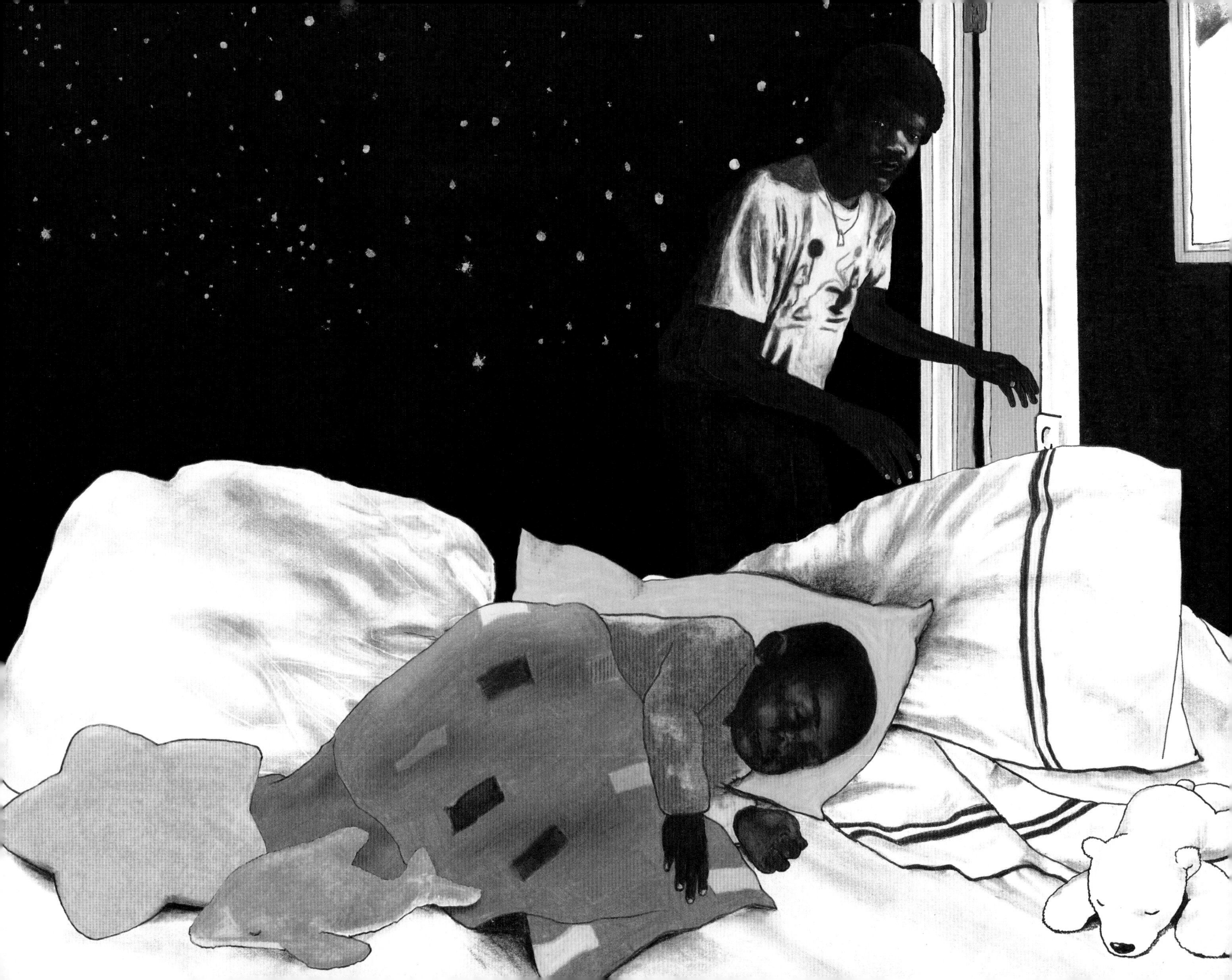

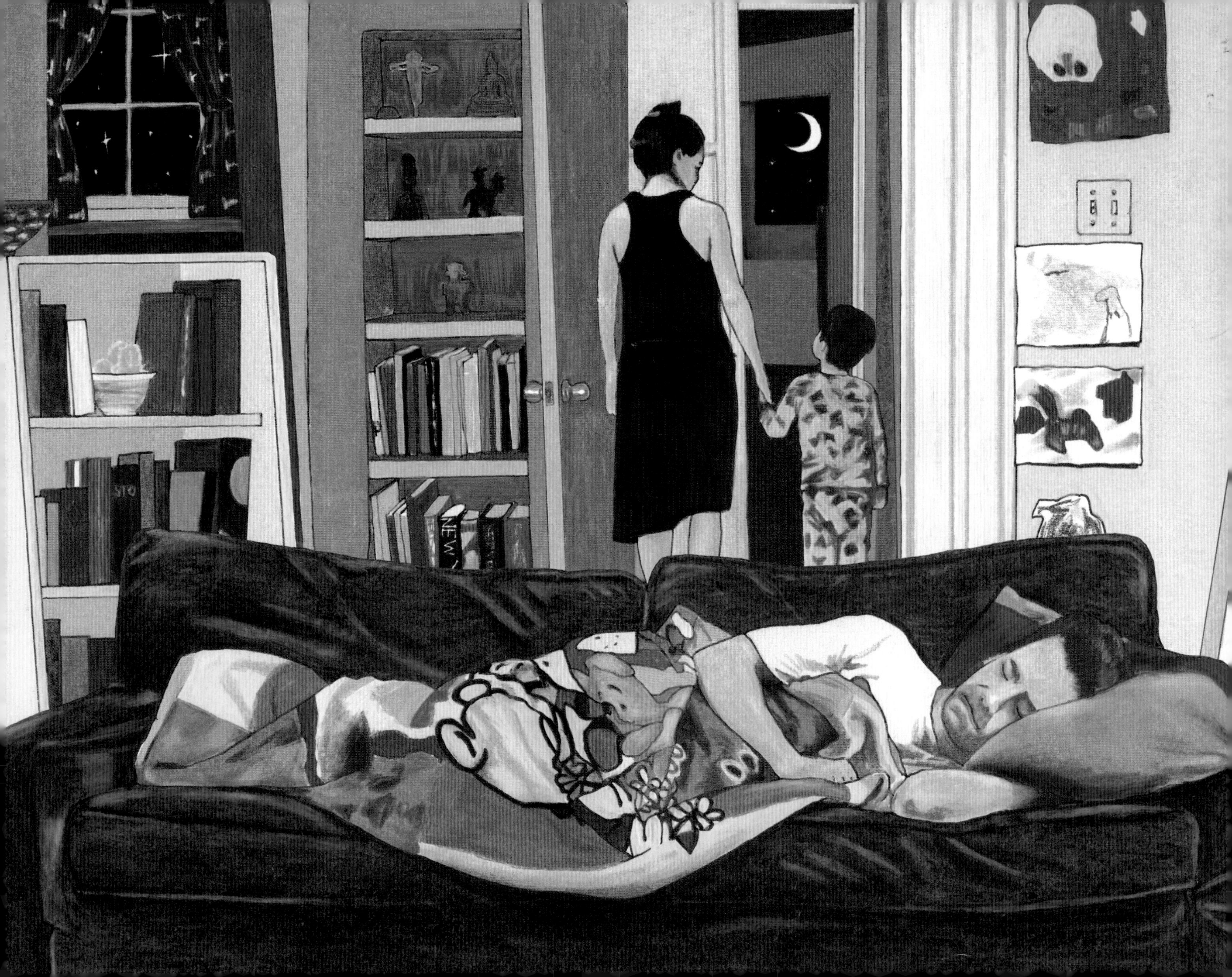

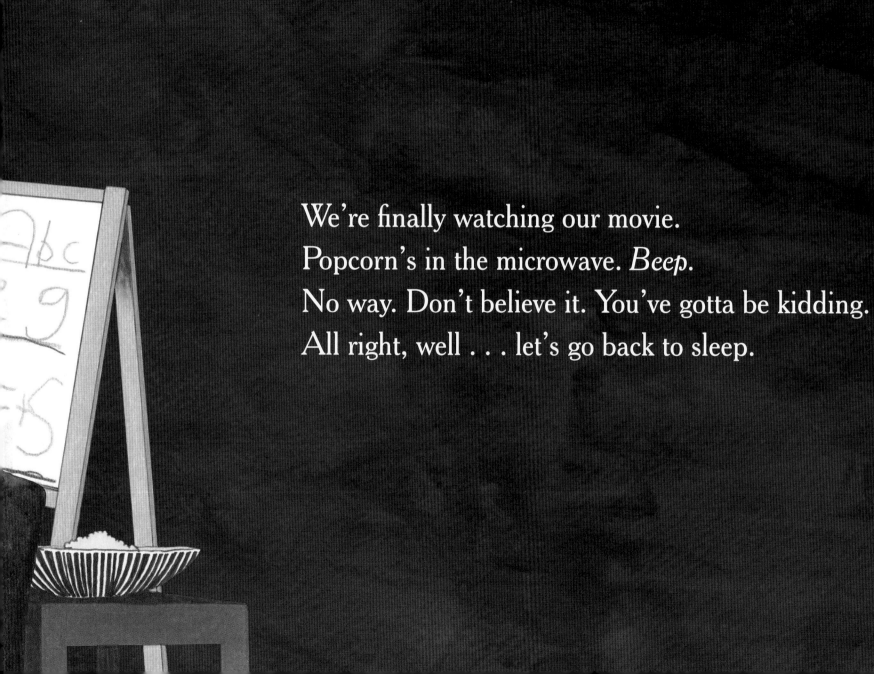

We're finally watching our movie.
Popcorn's in the microwave. *Beep.*
No way. Don't believe it. You've gotta be kidding.
All right, well . . . let's go back to sleep.

# The End